Dolphin Danger

Illus

For Tom Powell with lots of love

First published in the UK in 2010 by Usborne Publishing Ltd., Usborne House,
83-85 Saffron Hill, London EC1N 8RT, England. www.usborne.com

A CIP catalogue record for this book is available from the British Library.

FMAMJJASOND /10

ISBN 9781409506331 96095
Printed in Reading, Berkshire, UK.

Contents

Molly

Shanti

Eloise

Leila

Undersea Kingdom

Queen Luna

Aisha

Iona

Phoebe

Chapter One

Molly Holmes sat on her bed with her legs crossed, a pile of open books and papers spread out around her. Gusty rain beat against the windowpane and, glancing up, she could see dark storm clouds gathering over Horseshoe Bay. She shivered and pulled the thick red cardigan she was wearing tighter around her shoulders. She was glad that she and her family had come to live with Gran by the seaside, but as their cottage was all the way up on the cliff-top, you really felt the full force of the storms whenever they hit.

Molly turned her attention back to the books in front of her, trying to ignore the sound of the wind whistling in the chimney, and began leafing through the pages of a book Gran had lent her, called *Ocean Life*. Ahh – perfect.

A whole chapter on dolphins, with lots of beautiful photographs to look at. Molly's class at school was studying animals for their latest topic, and for their homework, they'd each been given a particular creature to find out about. "Write down lots of interesting facts about your animal, and then you can give a short presentation on your discoveries to the rest of the class," Mrs. Cartwright, Molly's teacher, had said.

Molly had been thrilled to be assigned the topic of "dolphins", as they were one of her favourite creatures – so beautiful and clever and fun.

She was lucky enough to have swum with dolphins many, many times, during her mermaid adventures...although she wasn't going to mention *that* particular fact in her homework, of course!

She sighed a little wistfully, not really looking forward to giving the presentation in front of the rest of the class. She'd been at Horseshoe Bay Primary School for two months now but still felt a bit of an outsider there. She knew already that she would be shy about standing up and speaking aloud to the others. What if she turned bright red and couldn't get her words out in the right order? What if everybody sniggered at her?

Her eye was caught by a picture on one page of the open book showing a pod of dolphins swimming along together. Lucky things, she thought, gazing at their smiley faces.

They didn't have to worry about feeling left-out, or being the new one, did they?

She picked up her pen and started to write.

Dolphins are playful, friendly creatures who live in groups and help each other to raise their babies (called calves) and get food, she began. *They are very fast swimmers (up to forty kilometres an hour) and love to leap in and out of the water...*

Molly paused and gazed out of the window at the sea, an anxious frown on her face. What the books and internet articles she'd read *didn't* say was that all the dolphins of the oceans had recently gone missing – and that Molly's mermaid friends had been desperately searching for them ever since...

For the last few months, since she and her family had moved to Gran's cottage in Horseshoe Bay, Molly had lived the most wonderful double life. She was the secret mermaid, the owner of a special piece of conch shell which magically turned her into a mermaid and took her to the ocean at night-time. But the last time Molly had become a mermaid, the Merqueen had given her some worrying news: that a number of different creatures had completely vanished from the seas. Queen Luna suspected some evil magic at work and Molly had immediately offered to help the Animal-Keeper mermaids search for the missing creatures.

Molly and Eloise, the mermaid who looked after the seahorses, had discovered the lost seahorses together and managed to set them free, but it had all been very mysterious. Molly was desperate to know if her mermaid friends had found the other missing creatures yet.

Molly glanced over at her shell necklace
which lay, as usual, on her bedside
table. Since the summer,
she'd had a special
"animal charm"
threaded onto it as
well – and the animal
charm had proved
every bit as magical
as the conch shell
when it came to saving
the seahorses. Molly wasn't
sure how it worked yet, but she really hoped
she'd find out before too long!

A few hours later, Molly was tucked up in bed,
feeling cosy and warm as the storm raged on
outside her window. Rain was still lashing

against the glass and she pulled the covers up higher around her ears, drowsily thinking about dolphins. Then she caught sight of a familiar soft pink light from her bedside table and her heart quickened – her magic shell was glowing! She closed her eyes, and in the very next moment she felt as if she were falling down, down, down. The special magic was working...she was being called to the mermaid world!

Seconds later, she sensed warm water against her skin and opened her eyes, a delicious feeling of excitement spreading through her. Yes! She was a mermaid again, down in the ocean with her very own beautiful green tail sparkling below her, and her shell necklace around her neck. A lobster scuttled by on the seabed, turning stalky eyes towards her with interest, before vanishing in a clump

of swaying emerald seaweed. Pretty white
scallop shells gleamed where they lay on the
golden sand.

Molly happily flipped her tail fin to and fro
and was sent somersaulting through the water,
with bubbles swirling all around her. Being a
mermaid was such fun!

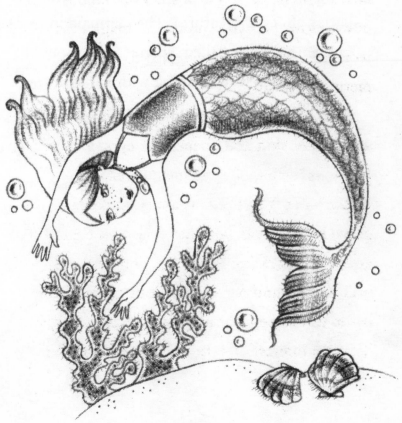

"Hey! Molly! Is that you?" came a shout, and Molly looked around to see a dark-haired mermaid swimming towards her.

Molly waved in recognition. "Hello!" she called. Last time she'd been here in the Undersea Kingdom, Molly had met all six of the special Animal-Keeper mermaids who protected various species of ocean creatures. The mermaid in front of her now was called Aisha. Molly thought she looked very striking with her shiny black bobbed hair, cut in a sharp fringe.

Her eyes were deep brown and almond-shaped, and she wore a bright pink top patterned with small pieces of orange shell.

The Animal-Keeper mermaids looked after one type of animal each, and the six mermaids Molly had met looked after the seahorses, dolphins, penguins, whales, turtles and octopuses. Aisha was the dolphin mermaid, Molly remembered, spotting the silver dolphin charm that hung around Aisha's neck.

"It's wonderful to see you," said Molly eagerly. "How are you?"

Aisha gave a friendly smile. "I'm good, thanks," she replied. "Eloise told us how you two rescued the seahorses together – good stuff! You did a great job!" Then her face fell. "I still haven't found my dolphins though, and I've been searching everywhere for two days now. I'm starting to worry something terrible has happened to them."

Molly bit her lip. "Has there been no sign of them at all?" she asked.

Aisha shook her head. "Not a thing," she said. "I got really excited earlier when I met a group of seals – they said they'd thought they'd heard some dolphin noises in this part of the ocean. Very very faint, they said. I was so relieved and happy I rushed straight here...but I've searched all over this area now and still haven't found a thing, let alone thousands of dolphins! The seals must have got muddled up, bless them. I'm sure they were only trying to help but..." She shrugged. "I'm so disappointed!"

Molly gave her a hug. Poor Aisha did look miserable. "Maybe we could go together to a different part of the ocean and—" she began, but then broke off, and listened hard. Was that a tiny clicking noise she had just heard? She strained her ears and caught the faint sound of high-pitched whistling. "Wait," she gasped. "I'm sure I just heard something. Listen!"

Chapter Two

Molly and Aisha both listened hard for a few moments, but there was no sound to be heard now. Molly blushed, wondering if she'd imagined the noises or been wrong, like the seals. "Sorry," she said. "I thought there was a clicking sound." She saw the lobster again and noticed how his pincers tapped together as he ran across the seabed. "Must have been something else," she mumbled, feeling embarrassed.

Aisha sighed. "No worries," she said, but now she looked disappointed once more. She raked a hand through her glossy hair then forced a smile. "Come on, let's go somewhere else."

Molly hesitated. If the seals had thought they'd heard something and she had too, shouldn't they explore every bit of this area, just to double-check? Perhaps there was a well-disguised underground cave where the dolphins had been hidden, or some other clue.

"Maybe..." she started, but Aisha was already swimming away.

"Come on," Aisha said. "I've looked everywhere, and they're not here. Let's keep moving."

Molly followed Aisha a little reluctantly, because her instincts told her to stay. They hadn't gone very far at all though, when she heard the clicking sound again.

It was very faint, as before – but as Molly listened, she was sure the tiny clicks and whistles sounded like dolphin noises. She turned to Aisha to see her friend's face alight with excitement. Aisha clutched Molly's arm. "I heard them! I heard them!" she cried. "Yes – those are definitely dolphin sounds!"

As Molly listened again, she realized something. She could *understand* what the dolphins were saying. "Help us! Help us!" their tiny voices called plaintively. "Help us!"

Molly felt a shiver run through her at their words, then noticed that her animal charm was shining extra brightly on her necklace. A friendly walrus had given Molly the animal charm as a thank-you gift for helping so many sea creatures when Molly and the other Shell-Keeper mermaids had defeated the evil Dark Queen Carlotta, back in the summer. The

walrus had told her that
wearing the charm
meant she'd be
helped by any
creature if she was
ever in trouble
while in the sea.
She twisted it
between her fingers
now and saw that a
dolphin hologram had
appeared on the metal.

"I think the sound is coming from this
direction," Aisha said at that moment, and
Molly snapped out of her thoughts to see Aisha
pointing towards a sandy hillock a short
distance away. "But it's weird that we can't see
any sign of the dolphins! They must be hidden
really well somewhere."

Molly nodded. "Maybe," she said. "The seahorses were absolutely tiny when Eloise and I found them. They'd been magically shrunk down so small you could hardly see them, and trapped in a sort of bubble. Whoever took the creatures can work powerful magic, so the dolphins could be tiny – or invisible – or anything!" She stared around, feeling tingly with excitement at the thought of finding all the dolphins. Thank goodness she and Aisha hadn't swum out of earshot!

"Come on, let's have a hunt around," Aisha said, swimming close to the seabed and running

her hand through the fine white sand there.
"Let's check out *everything*."

The two mermaids began searching. Molly
dived down to a bushy seaweed plant and began
leafing through its flat, slippery strands, hoping
to see something unusual that might be a clue,
or a link to the dolphins.

There was nothing in the seaweed, though, so she began searching through a pile of stones and shells, getting a shock when one of them shouted at her. "Put me down!" the shell cried indignantly, and several pink spined legs shot out and waved in the water.

"Oh!" cried Molly, startled. "Sorry," she said, realizing that there was a hermit crab inside the shell.

"I didn't realize anyone lived in there. I'm looking for some dolphins, have you seen any around here?"

The hermit crab wiggled its black beady eyes. "Seen any dolphins? As a matter of fact, I have. Well, sort of. If you can call 'em that, I mean."

He paused, and Molly felt her heart quicken. "Go on," she urged the crab.

"Well, I was looking for a new home, see," he said. "Me old shell was getting a bit of a squeeze. And I found this lovely big shell, ever so roomy it would have been for me, but it was all sealed off, wasn't it? Some kind of special doorway on it. Bit weird, frankly, you don't usually get that with shells. Not in this ocean. Anyway, what I'm trying to say is that the shell had already been nabbed by a load of baby dolphins. Ever so titchy, they were, more like shrimp than dolphins, but..."

Molly gasped. A shell with tiny dolphins in? This sounded promising. She and Aisha *had* to find it. "Where did you see this shell? Can you remember?"

The hermit pointed a claw, then frowned. "Oh," it said, staring into the distance. "It's gone. It was over there. But...it's vanished."

"Thank you," Molly said quickly, setting the crab down on the sand again. "We'll have a good look for it. Thank you *very* much!"

She swam over to Aisha and told her what she'd just heard. "The crab was pointing over at that sandy hillock," she said. "But it couldn't see the shell any more. I think we should dig around in the sand a bit. Maybe it's been buried."

"Brilliant," Aisha said enthusiastically, dimples flashing in her cheeks as she smiled. "Come on!"

The two mermaids swam towards the sandy hillock but just as they reached it, Molly almost

screamed in shock. The hillock had moved –
and was now rising up from the seabed before
her very eyes!

She backed away from it immediately,
feeling afraid. During the seahorse rescue, she
and Eloise had been frightened by some kind
of sand-monster which seemed to be guarding
the seahorses. Was this another of the scary
guards? "Aisha – watch out!" she cried. "I
think it might be a sand-monster!"

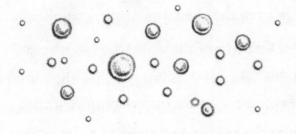

Chapter Three

"Me? A monster?" came a rasping, amused-sounding voice. "Well, that's just charming, isn't it? Lucky I'm not the type to take offence."

Aisha had been looking rather shaken but giggled now as she realized Molly's mistake. "It's a manta ray," she told Molly. "Perfectly safe."

Molly stared at the manta ray as it floated before them. It was absolutely enormous – about six or seven metres across, she estimated – and a sort of kite shape, with enormous wing-like fins at each side, a thin tail, and eyes which were set wide apart. It rippled with a smooth, flowing motion as if flapping mighty wings, and Molly felt herself blush. "I'm s-sorry," she said, rather taken aback. "It's just...I've never seen quite such a majestic ray as you before."

The manta ray gave a rich chuckle and floated up higher as it did so, before sinking slowly back to the seabed. "Good answer!" it replied. "Majestic – oh, I like that!" Then it noticed Molly's silver charm and looked at it with interest. "Aha! A very special mermaid, I see." It swished one of its large fins beneath its body with a flourish, as if making a bow. "I am at your service. Can I help you at all? Looking for something, are you?"

"You could say," Aisha put in. "Thousands of dolphins trapped in a shell. Yes, I know it sounds mad," she went on, as the manta ray looked disbelieving. "But an enchantment was put on the seahorses which made them shrink to miniature sizes, and we're guessing the same could have happened to the dolphins. We think they might be somewhere nearby."

The manta ray tilted its mighty head slightly as if thinking. "Well, I *have* heard some strange noises around here," it said, rising up in the water, then down again. "And—"

Molly's ears pricked up. As the ray had lifted off the seabed, the dolphin noises had suddenly become much louder. And then, when it lowered itself back down, the sounds became more muffled again. "Wait a minute," she said, interrupting the ray. "Would you mind swimming up again, please?"

"Up, up and away!" the ray said obligingly, swishing his fins down so that he was propelled higher in the water.

"Listen – can you hear? The dolphins' voices are louder," Molly said to Aisha. "I can hear them clearer now, can't you?"

"Yes," Aisha agreed excitedly, diving down to the area of the seabed where the ray had been. "They must be somewhere around here." She grinned and called up to the ray, who was floating high above them. "I think you might have been sitting on my dolphins, you know!"

Molly noticed a large white shell, with a curving, rounded shape. She went to pick it up but was surprised by how heavy it was. Using both hands, she managed to turn it over carefully and saw that it glimmered with mother-of-pearl inside. And there was something else...

"Aisha!" she gasped. "Come and look! There's something really weird about this shell."

Aisha swam over at once and Molly showed her how the mouth of the shell had been sealed over with what looked like a sheet of glass.

"Let's see," Aisha said, moving the shell into the light. Then her mouth formed a little "o" of surprise. "Wow!" she cried. "Oh, look! The crab was right!"

Molly peered over. "The dolphins!" she cried, delighted to see them there. But oh, how different they were to their usual beautiful, playful selves. Beneath the glassy seal, hordes of tiny little dolphin-shaped specks moved about in water. If you didn't know better, you might think they were just floating grains of sand, but both Molly and Aisha could hear the dolphins' clicks and whistles even louder and clearer now, and were quite sure of what they were looking at.

"They've been shrunk, just like the seahorses," Molly said. "The poor things. Who can be doing this?"

Aisha bit her lip. "And why?" she burst out. "Why would anyone want to trap them in a shell prison? What have the dolphins ever done to anybody to deserve this?" Her fingers were trembling with rage as she held the shell. "Well, I'm going to get them out of here," she said, and pressed her thumbs against the glassy covering. "If I can...just... break...this..." Her fingernails clicked against the smooth surface but it didn't break, even when she tried knocking at it

with a small rock. "It's completely solid," she wailed.

Molly opened her mouth to reply but before she could say a single word, the seabed below them began rippling and churning.

"What's happening?" Aisha yelled, holding tight to the shell.

A mist of gritty sand was swirling all around them and then, up from the seabed, rose a sinister, looming form. Molly stared in horror.

Through the blizzard of sand, she could see that the monster was tall and towering, and vaguely human-shaped. It had two red eyes shining out of its head and a thick, powerful-looking body with two strong arms and solidly built thighs.

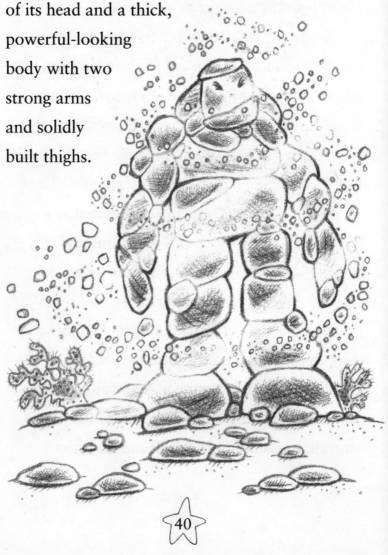

It also seemed to be made entirely of *rock*, Molly realized. Fear washed through her as the monster lunged for her, its arm making a horrible grating sound as it moved.

"Swim for it!" shouted Molly desperately, but before she or Aisha could turn, the monster had snatched the white shell full of dolphins from Aisha's hands with a single sweeping movement, then sunk back into the seabed with it, all in a single heartbeat.

"No – give that back!" Molly yelled, scrabbling at the sand, and trying to blink the grit out of her eyes. But the monster had completely vanished, taking the large shell with it, and despite Molly's and Aisha's best efforts, they couldn't find any trace of it.

The sand blizzard had settled now, and the two mermaids stared at each other in dismay.

"That was horrible." Aisha shivered,

rubbing her arms. "I've never seen anything like it before. The way it just *appeared* from the sand so suddenly. And it was so strong too, snatching the shell from me like that."

"It was a different monster from the last one," Molly said in a low voice. "That was made of sand, not rock, and didn't seem so big either. Where are these monsters coming from?" She took a deep breath. "Well, we can't give up now. Not now we know the dolphins are trapped in that shell. We've got to find it again!"

The two mermaids carried on scraping and digging at the sand in the hope of seeing the white shell again – but found nothing. It was nerve-racking, raking through the sand with their fingers, especially as they knew that the rock-monster was somewhere below them. The thought of it grabbing her and pulling her down under the sand gave Molly the shivers.

"Oh, it's no good," Aisha muttered after a while, throwing a white rock over her shoulder in frustration. "We could be here for hours searching."

"Maybe you two need a little fin power," said the voice of the manta ray, and Molly saw it was gliding down towards them again. He winked at them and smiled. "Want me to try?"

"Oh, yes please," said Molly at once. Her fingernails were nearly all broken by now.

The manta ray positioned itself carefully, then flapped its mighty flat sides with great force. And then... Whoosh! A great current of water was created, washing a tide of sand and mud away from the area where the monster had disappeared.

"Oops," it said, as Molly and Aisha were showered with mud and small pebbles. "Sorry. Should have warned you I was going to do that."

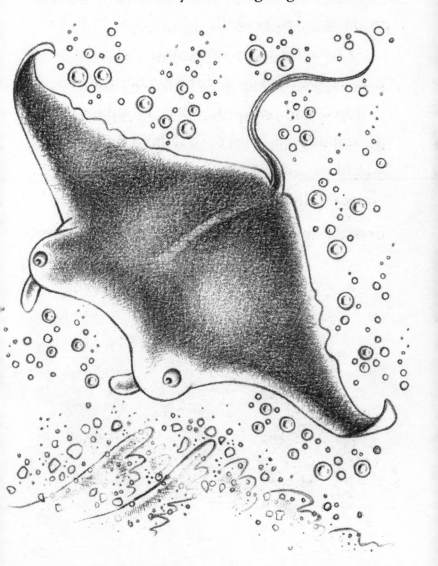

Molly wiped the splatters from her face and shook out her hair. The sand was gradually settling around them, but there was still no sign of the large white shell.

"One more time," the manta ray said. "Move aside, ladies, I'm going for a big one this time."

Molly and Aisha backed away and the ray gave another huge swoosh of his fins. It really was like seeing an enormous bird flying in the water, Molly thought in delight. Whoosh! A

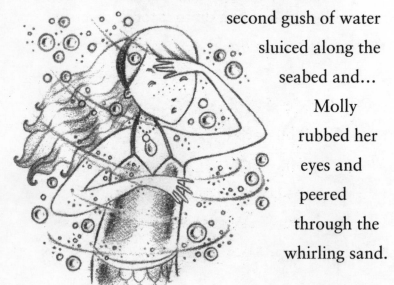

second gush of water sluiced along the seabed and…

Molly rubbed her eyes and peered through the whirling sand.

What was that? Had she really just seen a flash of white half-buried in the seabed?

She dived down through the water. Yes! There was the shell – the manta ray had found it!

"Here!" she cried, grabbing at it eagerly... but something seemed to be gripping the other end of the shell from beneath the seabed. A shudder of fear ran through her. "Oh no," she hissed to Aisha. "I think the rock-monster's holding on to it too!"

"Pull it!" Aisha urged. "As hard as you can!"

Molly tugged at the shell with every bit of her strength but it didn't give at all. In fact, to Molly's alarm, she felt the shell move deeper into the seabed, pulling her down with it!

"Aisha, help!" she gasped, having visions of being dragged right under.

Aisha took hold of
Molly around her
middle and the
two mermaids
pulled hard
together. They
heaved and
heaved with
all their might
until at last,
with a sucking
noise, the shell
suddenly came
free.

"Got it!"
Molly cheered
in relief. Then, heart pounding, she turned tail
and began to swim off, hoping she could get
away before the monster-creature came after her.

But already she could feel a cold shadow falling on her, and a rushing movement behind her and she knew, with a sick lurch, that she was being chased. She could hear the monster's rocky legs clattering as it ran after her in great strides. "Go faster, Molly!" she heard Aisha scream. "Swim faster!"

It was hard work, swimming fast while holding on to the large, heavy shell. Glancing over her shoulder, Molly saw that the dark figure of the monster was closing in on her. It was stretching a long, strong arm towards her and she caught sight of sharp yellow claws at the end of its stony fingers. "Swim faster!" she urged herself desperately, but it was too late. A cold, hard hand reached around her tail...

Chapter Four

"Swim faster!" Molly said to herself again, almost sobbing with fear. And then a strange thing happened. Her silver animal charm suddenly felt very hot against her skin and then…and then… Whoosh!

"Whooooaaaa!" she screamed in surprise. All of a sudden she was whizzing through the water at super-speed, faster than she'd ever swum before. The monster clung on to her tailfin but with one sharp flick, she managed to throw him off, and powered along even faster, moving at an incredible rate. The seabed was a blur beneath her, her whole body taut and strong as she shot along.

It wasn't long before she'd left the monster – and Aisha – way behind, and once she felt a safe distance from them, Molly finally slowed to a stop. Her tail was tingling from going so fast, but she felt full of energy, as if she could do it all over again. "Wow," she murmured to herself, leaning against a large boulder, suddenly giddy. "How did that happen?" She peered into the shell where the dolphin-specks were still whizzing around. "Are you guys all right in there?" she asked. "I didn't go too fast for you, did I?"

Then she smiled at the question. No – dolphins were really fast swimmers themselves, of course. They probably felt right at home racing along at super-speed.

She could see a figure approaching in the distance and tensed for a moment until she realized that the silky black hair and bright pink top could only belong to Aisha. "Hey!" the mermaid called breathlessly as she drew nearer. "That was some swim, Molly. Amazing. I didn't know you could go so fast!"

Molly grinned, feeling a little sheepish. "Neither did I," she admitted. "I don't know how I did it. I was saying to myself, *Go faster!* and then off I went. But it seemed *magically* fast, if you know what I mean. Faster than I've ever swum before."

Aisha cocked her head. "It *looked* magically fast, too," she said. "The monster didn't stand a chance of catching up with you. Luckily for me, it was so intent on catching *you*, I managed to slip away unnoticed." Then she pointed. "Hey, what's happened to your charm, Molly? It's shining so brightly!"

Molly looked down. Aisha was right. Her silver animal charm was sparkling white-silver, and when she lifted it, it felt very hot to the touch. She flipped it over and saw the dolphin hologram on the other side again. "I'm starting to think there's some really powerful magic in this charm," she said thoughtfully. "Last time,

when Eloise and I were trying to free the seahorses, I sort of disappeared – or rather, my whole body and face turned the colour of the rocks behind me, so that I blended in, and was hidden from the monster."

Aisha's eyes glittered with excitement. "And that was the charm's magic, do you think?"

"I don't know," Molly replied uncertainly. "It's very odd, isn't it?" She remembered the shell full of dolphins then. "One thing I *do* know is that we should try to set these dolphins free before another monster pops up. There might be more of them, lurking beneath the seabed."

"Brrr." Aisha shivered, looking uneasy at the thought. Then she peered into the shell. "So… how are we going to get you little guys out?"

They both looked at the shell, trying to think of ideas. "A crab managed to break open the bubble where the seahorses were trapped,"

Molly said. "I wonder if there are any crabs around here who would help us, like before?"

They gazed around hopefully but this particular part of the sea was deserted. There were no crabs or lobsters to be seen, and no other creatures either. Molly looked upwards too, just in case she could see a friendly shark who might offer assistance – their strong, jagged teeth would surely be able to crack open the shell – but she could only see a couple of seagulls floating on top of the water. "I'm sure there must be a crab around here *somewhere*," Aisha was saying, but just then, a better idea popped into Molly's head.

"Seagulls have very sharp beaks, don't they?" she asked. "Maybe a seagull could break into the shell with their beak by pecking at it. Come on, let's swim up to the surface and ask one. It's worth a try."

Aisha agreed, so the two mermaids swam up, holding the shell between them. "Uh-oh," Aisha whispered as they surfaced. "They're asleep."

Molly glanced at the two birds who were sitting motionless on the surface of the water, their heads tucked beneath smooth white wings. Then her gaze flicked to the horizon. A faint pink line of light was visible and she knew that dawn wasn't far away. The morning sunrise

always marked the end of Molly's mermaid
adventure for that particular night and she
would be magically returned to her own bed.
She had to help Aisha free the dolphins before
then – she couldn't bear the thought of leaving
while they were still trapped! "We'll just
have to wake one of them up," she hissed.
"They won't mind, will they? It is an
emergency."

Aisha bit her lip. "Seagulls are *so* bad-tempered," she whispered. "We'll be lucky if they don't start pecking *us* instead of the shell."

Molly shrugged. "We don't have a choice," she said, and gently prodded the nearest seagull. "Um...excuse me?" she said politely.

The seagull gave an indignant squawk, shook out huge wings with a loud flap and glared at Molly with beady eyes. "What on earth—?" it shrieked crossly. "Have you any idea what *time* it is?" Then it stared at Molly's charm and gulped, blinking a few times in surprise.

"Oh," it said, in a more reverent voice, and nudged at its neighbour. "Hey – wake up. There's a mermaid here with the animal charm. I said, wake up!"

The second seagull awoke with a furious screech and lashed out at the first with its wing. "What do you think you're playing at?" it complained. Then it saw Molly's animal charm and abruptly lowered its wings. "Yes?" it asked in a quieter voice.

"Um... Hi," Molly said, slightly

nervous of the grumpy seagulls but relieved
that they seemed to respect her animal charm
at least. "We were wondering if you could
have a go at breaking this shell with your
beaks, please? If you don't mind, of course."

"Not at all, not at all," the first seagull
said in its peculiar squawky voice. "Let's have
a look."

Molly and Aisha held the shell towards it,
and the seagull pecked obligingly at the glassy
covering that was trapping the dolphins.

"Hmmm," said the seagull. "It's tough.

My beak's as good as they get, but it stands no chance. Maybe we need to try the clam trick."

"The clam trick?" Molly echoed uncertainly.

The second seagull nodded. "Sure," it said. "Tried and tested many times. Are you saying you've never seen a seagull break open a clamshell?"

Molly shook her head. The seagulls laughed, a high-pitched, screechy sort of sound. "Honey, prepare to be impressed," the first said. And with that, the seagulls took off high up into the sky with the shell held between their beaks.

"Wait – what are you doing?" Molly cried in alarm. "Bring that back!"

"Oh, no! They're heading for those rocks," Aisha realized. "That's how they smash open clam shells – by flying up high and dropping them onto rocks." She clapped a hand to her face anxiously. "Which is all very well, if they're going to eat the clam, but I don't want my dolphins to get hurt – or eaten! Quick – we've got to stop them!"

But just as the words left her lips, the seagulls let go of the white shell above the rocks. Molly and Aisha were too late to do anything and could only watch the shell hurtling down through the half-light before landing with a sickening crack on the rocks.

Chapter Five

"Oh my goodness," Aisha gasped, throwing herself forwards in the water and swimming over to the rocks. "That sounded bad."

Molly followed, wishing she hadn't asked the seagulls to help in the first place. What if the dolphins had all been hurt because of her stupid idea? Or, even worse, what if they'd been *killed*?

Just as she reached the rocks, the seagulls swooped down and, with a triumphant squawk each, pushed the shell over the bumpy rocks towards Aisha and Molly. "There!" one screeched. "No problemo!"

Molly caught hold of the shell, and her hands trembled as she turned it over. The hard glassy substance that had kept the dolphins trapped inside the shell had split, and a watery liquid was seeping between the cracks. One of the

seagulls leaned over, deftly plucked the cracked pieces of glass – or whatever it was – out of the shell and tossed them into the sea.

The watery liquid came streaming out of the white shell, and with it, all of the thousands of tiny, speck-like dolphins. As they tumbled into the sea, they began to grow and grow and *grow* until they were full-size dolphins once more. Soon the water around Molly and Aisha was absolutely teeming with the silver-grey bodies of bottlenose dolphins, spotted dolphins, white-sided dolphins, beautiful blue spinner dolphins... Molly recognized them and many other types from her homework project. She stared around, feeling utterly thrilled that the dolphins were free again. They'd done it!

Aisha was welcoming and greeting all the dolphins in turn, wrapping her arms around their slippery bodies with tears in her eyes.

"You should all thank these guys," she said, gesturing to the seagulls. "They're the ones who got you out of that shell!"

The dolphins seemed confused. "What shell? What are you talking about?" they asked Aisha, their friendly faces blank.

Aisha seemed surprised at their questions. "*That* shell!" she replied, pointing at where it had fallen down to the seabed.

"Don't you remember? You were all tiny and trapped inside. And who put you in there anyway? Was it a sort of rock-monster creature?"

The dolphins exchanged glances, seeming utterly perplexed. "I don't know what you mean," one said after a few moments. "Trapped in a shell? But *we* couldn't fit in *that*!"

Molly remembered the seahorses being equally confused when they'd been released, and led Aisha to one side. "They don't remember," she said quietly.

Aisha was watching a pod of dolphins swimming sedately away. "And it's not just that," she said. "Look at the way they're moving. Usually they're so joyful and energetic, leaping out of the water, bucking and soaring. Now... There's something not quite right about them." She sighed, then squared her shoulders. "Maybe they just need a bit of encouragement," she said, clapping her hands. "Hey, you guys! Who wants a game of Tag? I'm It. Three... two...one...coming to get you!"

The dolphins rushed away, giggling as Aisha threw herself after them.

"Can't catch me!"

"Over here!"

"Too slow!" they called out, dodging Aisha
as she whirled about, trying to tag one of them.
Molly joined in too, and couldn't stop smiling.

It was wonderful to hear the dolphins clicking and whistling with excitement as they darted through the water like silver streaks. But although they were all having fun now, they still weren't as speedy as usual, and Aisha found it easy work to tag a spinner dolphin on the tail.

Aisha came over, laughing, as the game got rowdier. "Well, they're happy at least," she said. "Oh, it's lovely to play with them again. I've missed them."

Molly smiled. "I bet," she said. Maybe it would just take some time for the effects of the enchantment to wear off, she thought hopefully. With a bit of luck, the dolphins would regain their full speed before too long, and it would be as if the whole thing never happened.

Just as she was thinking this, a shaft of rosy-pink light struck the water in front of the girls. Molly looked up in dismay and saw that the red

sun was now inching up from the horizon and
the sky was flooded with early-morning light.
"Oh, no," she groaned. "I hate having to go so
soon." She could feel the familiar tugging
sensation inside her body, as if someone were
trying to reel her in on an invisible fishing line.

"Thank you, Molly," Aisha cried, throwing
her arms around her neck. "Thanks for
everything. You were brilliant – and I'm so happy
the dolphins are free. See you soon, I hope!"

"I hope so too!" Molly called. Then bubbles were whirling around her and she was being pulled, pulled, pulled...

Moments later, she felt her warm bed beneath her again, and blinked her eyes open. If only her adventures could last longer! And what would happen to the dolphins now? She and Aisha – and the seagulls – had released them from the shell, but would they be all right?

Her mind was racing with questions as she rolled onto her side. The house was silent; even her baby brother Toby seemed to still be asleep. Well, there was no way *she'd* be able to doze off again now, she thought to herself, pushing her hair out of her eyes and sitting up. Not when her brain was whirling and wondering.

She stretched her arms above her head, shivering as the cold morning air hit her skin.

Then she swung her legs out of bed, pulled on her thick purple dressing gown and padded over to her desk. The sun was creeping up higher into the sky, a glowing red disc, casting crimson reflections into the sea. The sky was gradually lightening, the darkness now streaked with soft pink and orange light, as if a giant paintbrush had been splashed across it.

Molly thought about all the dolphins she'd seen, the different shapes, colours and sizes of them, then picked up her pen and began to write.

"Thank you, Chloe, that was a wonderful presentation on whales," Mrs. Cartwright, Molly's teacher said, later that morning.

Chloe, a tall girl with messy brown plaits, beamed at the words of praise and sat down in her seat.

"Who shall we have next?" Mrs. Cartwright asked, her gaze moving around the class. "Perhaps we should go straight to another wonderful sea creature – the dolphin. Molly, would you like to stand up and tell us what you've found out about the dolphin, please?"

Molly got to her feet, her homework book in her hands. Her heart beat a little faster as she felt her classmates' eyes upon her. "Dolphins are mammals, not fish," she began. "They have lungs and breathe air…"

She was reading from her notes, but after a while she put the book down, and chose her own words as they came to her instead. "Dolphins are really friendly and cheeky," she said, smiling as she remembered the times she and her mermaid friends had played chase with them in the past. "They live in families and look after each other. You get all different sorts – the bottlenoses are the silvery-grey ones with stumpy beaks, and they're the dolphins you're most likely to see around Britain. But there are lots of other kinds – killer whales are

actually dolphins too," she went on, with a shy smile at Chloe.

The classroom was quiet; everyone was listening as Molly went on with her presentation. "And you get river dolphins as well, including this really cool pink dolphin called the Amazon river dolphin. What else? Oh yes." She smiled to herself. "Dolphins talk to each other using something called echolocation," she went on, then paused, thinking about how to describe it. "It's like finding things using echoes. The dolphins make clicking sounds like this."

Molly did a perfect impression of a dolphin's clicking noises and a few people tried to copy her. Nobody could do it quite as well as Molly, though!

"The sound of the dolphin's clicks bounces back to the dolphin, and then it can work out what's in its path," she went on. "It's really clever, because it means it can catch fish in the dark, and make its way easily through murky waters." She turned to her teacher. "And that's about it."

Mrs. Cartwright began clapping – and everyone joined in! Molly felt really proud of herself as she stood there, with the rest of the class smiling and applauding her. It felt great.

"Molly, that was fantastic," Mrs. Cartwright said. "Not only did you find out all sorts of interesting facts about dolphins, but you spoke so fluently and confidently while you told us about them. And as for that dolphin impression – it was marvellous. Anyone would think you'd been chatting to the dolphins for real!"

Molly sat down in her seat again, blushing. If only Mrs. Cartwright knew how right she was! What would she say to *that*?

Chloe, the tall girl, gave her a thumbs up from her seat nearby. "That was cool, Molly," she whispered.

"Thanks," Molly whispered back shyly.

She glanced out of the classroom window while Mrs. Cartwright decided whose turn it was to speak next. She could just see a slice of Horseshoe Bay over the grassy headland, where a low winter sun was sparkling on the ruffled waves. It was good to think that further out at sea, the dolphins would be swimming freely again, and hopefully back to their normal bouncy selves.

A pair of seagulls shrieked suddenly as they soared over the bay, and Molly felt tingly with happiness, remembering last night's magical mermaid adventure. How she hoped she'd be able to help the Animal-Keeper mermaids find more of the missing sea creatures…and that she wouldn't have to wait too long before her next visit to the Undersea Kingdom!

The End

The Secret Mermaid

Read on for a sneak preview of Molly's next magical underwater adventure...

Penguin Peril

Dad's words came back to Molly – about how he was glad he wasn't a polar bear or penguin – and a chill crept over her. She'd been called back to the Undersea Kingdom by the Merqueen recently because six different species – the seahorses, dolphins, penguins, whales, octopuses and turtles – had completely vanished from the oceans. Molly had vowed to help the Animal-Keeper mermaids, who each looked after a certain type of creature, to find them again, but so far it was proving very difficult. Not only had someone (or some*thing*) used dark magic to shrink the creatures to tiny sizes, making it almost impossible to track them down, but hostile monsters made from sand and rock had been guarding the missing creatures she'd found so far, which made the whole mission a lot more scary. Molly and her mermaid friends had been able to recover the missing seahorses and dolphins, and had managed to escape from the monsters each time, but she was already dreading meeting one of them again.

"Molly, come away from the window now, you're shivering," her mum said just then, and Molly obeyed, even though she knew it wasn't just the cold that was making her shiver. It was the thought of a sandy hand stretching towards her, trying to clutch her in its strong, cold grip...

She sat by the fire again hurriedly, trying to shake the image out of her mind.

That night, Molly settled down in bed, pulling the covers up high around her ears as she heard the wind battering the roof and chimney outside. She imagined snow falling soft as feathers onto the beach and hoped it was settling on the rocks and sand, like a delicate white blanket. Then, as she rolled over sleepily, she caught sight of her special shell necklace which she always kept on her bedside table. On the necklace was strung a creamy-pink piece of shell, as well as a silver animal charm she'd been given by a friendly walrus.

As she looked at it now, the shell started to glow, pulsing with pink and golden sparkles, twinkling with the promise of mermaid magic…

Molly shut her eyes quickly and a familiar tingling sensation went through her body. Then she felt as if she were dropping from a huge height – down, down, down. Moments later, she opened her eyes to find herself at the bottom of the ocean, with soft white sand below her and a tangle of coppery-brown seaweed billowing nearby. The water was cold and clear, and a couple of surprised-looking silver-grey cod were staring at her with huge round eyes.

"Whoa! Where did you just swim from?" one asked, blinking.

"You are *fast*, girl. We didn't even see you coming!" the other marvelled.

Molly beamed. "It's magic," she told them happily, flipping her beautiful green mermaid tail and turning a somersault in the water. Oh, she just loved being a mermaid!

"Magic?" the first fish echoed. "Aha. So you're the one who made that weird sparkly iceberg, are you?"

"Oh yes, the terns can't talk about anything else right now," the second put in. "The way they keep chattering on and on about it...goodness! It's enough to give you earache."

Molly frowned, not understanding. She knew that a tern was a kind of bird, but didn't know anything about a sparkly iceberg. "What do you mean?" she asked.

The first cod opened its mouth to reply, but another voice came first. "Hey! Molly, is that you?"

Molly spun around in a semicircle to see a smiling mermaid swimming towards her. It was Phoebe, one of the Animal-Keeper mermaids. She had brown wavy hair with a circlet of pink sea-flowers threaded through it, and she wore a green top with a sea-flower trim. Her tail was bright pink.

"Hi, Phoebe," Molly said, remembering that Phoebe was the mermaid who looked after all the penguins. "How are things? Any news?"

Phoebe shook her head sadly as she drew level with Molly. "Not really," she said. "I feel as if I've searched every crevice of ice in the whole of Antarctica, looking for my penguins, and I've still found nothing. I don't know where else to try."

Molly glanced back at the fish. "These guys were just telling me about a strange sparkling iceberg the terns have seen," she said. "Do you know anything about that?"

"A sparkling iceberg?" Phoebe shook her head, looking interested. "First I've heard of it," she said. "Where is it?"

The fish gave Phoebe directions and then swam off with a friendly wave of their fins. Phoebe turned to Molly, looking excited. "Sounds to me as if there could be something magical about this iceberg," she said. "Let's investigate!"

To find out what happens next, read

The Secret Mermaid

Penguin Peril

To find out more
about Molly and all her
mermaid friends, and have
some magical ocean fun,
check out

www.thesecretmermaid.co.uk

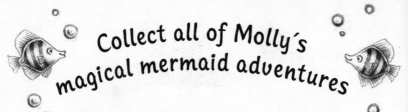

Collect all of Molly's magical mermaid adventures

Enchanted Shell ◎ 9780746096154

Molly is transported to the Undersea Kingdom for the first time, where she discovers she is the secret mermaid!

Seaside Adventure ◎ 9780746096161

To help Ella recover her piece of the magical conch, Molly must find a way to trap an angry killer whale.

Underwater Magic ◎ 9780746096178

Can Molly find some pirate treasure to win back Delphi's shell from a grumpy sea urchin?

Reef Rescue ◎ 9780746096192

Molly must help Coral find her shell to restore the ocean reefs, but a swarm of jellyfish stands in their way…

Deep Trouble ◎ 9780746096185

Pearl's conch piece is trapped in an undersea volcano and guarded by sea snakes. How can she and Molly release it?

Return of the Dark Queen ◎ 9780746096208

Molly must save Shivana from an Arctic prison before the Shell-Keeper mermaids can finally face the Dark Queen and complete the magical conch.

Seahorse SOS ⦿ 9781409506324

There's more trouble in the Undersea Kingdom and
Molly joins in the search for the missing seahorses.

Dolphin Danger ⦿ 9781409506331

Molly and Aisha can hear faint calls for help but the
dolphins are nowhere to be seen. Where can they be?

Penguin Peril ⦿ 9781409506348

Could the Dark Queen be behind the mysterious
disappearance of the penguins from the icy seas?

Turtle Trouble ⦿ 9781409506355

There are some scary monsters lurking in the coral reef and
they're guarding the turtles Molly has come to set free!

Whale Rescue ⦿ 9781409506393

Molly must not only save the trapped whales but also
her mermaid friend, Leila.

The Dark Queen's Revenge ⦿ 9781409506409

The Dark Queen is back and she wants to rule the
Undersea Kingdom with her bad magic. Can Molly put
an end to her vile plans?

For more enchanting adventures
log on to
www.fiction.usborne.com